CONQUERING ANOREXIA

CONQUERING ANOREXIA

KATHERINE WALDEN AND STEPHANIE WATSON

Rosen Publishing
New York

Published in 2016 by The Rosen Publishing Group, Inc.
29 East 21st Street, New York, NY 10010

Copyright © 2016 by The Rosen Publishing Group, Inc.

First Edition

All rights reserved. No part of this book may be reproduced in any form without permission in writing from the publisher, except by a reviewer.

Library of Congress Cataloging in Publication Data

Walden, Katherine, author.
 Conquering anorexia / Katherine Walden and Stephanie Watson. — First edition.
     pages cm. — (Conquering eating disorders)
 Audience: Grades 7–12.
 Includes bibliographical references and index.
 ISBN 978-1-4994-6203-6 (library bound)
 1. Anorexia nervosa—Juvenile literature. 2. Anorexia nervosa—Treatment—Juvenile literature. I. Watson, Stephanie, 1969– author. II. Title.
 RC552.A5W35 2016
 616.85'262—dc23

2015017870

For many of the images in this book, the people photographed are models. The depictions do not imply actual situations or events.

Manufactured in the United States of America

CONTENTS

7   CHAPTER ONE
An Eating Disorder

18   CHAPTER TWO
The Roots of Anorexia

29   CHAPTER THREE
Combatting Risk Factors

37   CHAPTER FOUR
Symptoms of Anorexia

45   CHAPTER FIVE
The Recovery Process

54   GLOSSARY

56   FOR MORE INFORMATION

60   FOR FURTHER READING

62   INDEX

An Eating Disorder

CHAPTER ONE

The word "anorexia" literally means "loss of appetite." But anorexia is more like self-starvation—becoming so obsessed with losing weight and dieting that you ignore your body's hunger signals. Although people with anorexia are always hungry, they take pride in denying hunger, feeling more in control and independent. This belief has very dangerous consequences. If anorexia progresses far enough, you can lose massive amounts of body weight—enough to cause psychological problems, physical problems, and even death.

Anorexia is a very serious condition. An article in the December 2009 issue of *The American Journal of Psychiatry* reported that 4 percent of people who are anorexic die as a result of the disease. While anyone can develop anorexia, the group that is most at risk of doing so is young women. In the last decade, health care professionals have found that the disease has become increasingly common in girls under the age of thirteen.

You may have heard the term "anorexia" used before. Maybe you talked about it in health class, read about it in a magazine, or heard that a celebrity is suffering from the disease. Chances are, anorexia or another eating-related issue probably influences your life or that of a family member or friend right now. You, he, or she might already feel a few of the forces that cause

This young man is in recovery from anorexia. The disease's full name is actually anorexia nervosa. It is a serious, at times even fatal, illness.

an eating disorder to kick in: insecurity, peer pressure, and society's pressure to be thin.

Though anorexia is a serious disease, a meaningful recovery is possible. Doctors are slowly beginning to better understand anorexia. There are now treatments that can help people who have anorexia gain self-esteem and get healthy.

Healthy and Disordered Eating

Everybody needs food in order to survive and grow. But eating also often has emotional and social importance for people. It's how people bond with each other on holidays, at the movies, and at home. And sometimes there are expectations, even pressures, about what and how much you eat.

If you have a healthy relationship with food, you're able to eat when you are hungry and enjoy what you eat. If you don't have a healthy relationship with food, eating can cause discomfort, guilt, conflicts with others, and even self-hatred.

An eating disorder usually arises when other influences, such as low self-esteem, abuse in the home, or peer pressure, contribute to food becoming an avenue to control something in a person's life or a symptom of other things that might be happening in a person's life. These negative feelings about food become overwhelming enough to interfere with your health and nutrition. Your eating becomes "disordered," causing both physical and emotional troubles. Along with anorexia, the most common eating disorders people are diagnosed with are bulimia, binge eating disorder, and OSFED (which is short for Other Specified Feeding and Eating Disorder).

According to a study that was published by the National Institute of Mental Health in 2010, 2.7 percent of teens between the ages of thirteen and eighteen suffer from an eating disorder. While the

People with anorexia and other eating disorders spend a lot of their time thinking about—and, in the case of anorexia, trying to avoid—food.

majority of people with eating disorders are female, the number of males who are suffering from them is increasing. There are many men and boys who go undiagnosed either because of the lack of reporting the disorder or because of misdiagnoses.

Bulimia

People who suffer from bulimia nervosa—often shortened to just bulimia—binge (eat a large quantity of food in a short time) and then purge (eliminate the food, usually by vomiting, using laxatives, or taking diuretics, also known as water pills). The self-esteem of people with bulimia is unhealthily dependent on their weight or body shape. Unlike people with anorexia, though, people with bulimia are not necessarily underweight.

Bulimia does major damage to the body. It can cause ulcers (holes or tears) in the stomach, throat, and mouth. People with bulimia can develop yellow, damaged teeth from the acids brought up into the mouth through repeated vomiting. Abusing laxatives causes painful stomach cramps and weakens the digestive system.

Binge Eating Disorder

People suffering from binge eating disorder eat uncontrollably but don't purge afterward. They consume large amounts of food very quickly whether or not they feel hungry. They usually do this in private and feel unable to control how much or what they eat. People who regularly overeat may forget how to read their body's normal hunger signals and may not know how to satisfy them.

Binge eating is a feature of several eating disorders. It is a key aspect of both bulimia and binge eating disorder. Some people with anorexia binge eat, too, later purging the food they ate.

OSFED

People whose symptoms do not allow them to be diagnosed with anorexia, bulimia, or binge eating disorder may be diagnosed with Other Specified Feeding and Eating Disorder—often known by its acronym, OSFED. It has several subtypes, including atypical anorexia—in which a patient demonstrates many of the features of anorexia but is not significantly underweight.

Anyone Can Develop Anorexia

Anyone—male or female, young or old, and from all walks of life—can get anorexia. However, the disease is more common in teens than in adults. It usually sets in before the age of twenty-five. There is also a higher rate of anorexia among females than among males. This may be because society puts much more pressure on young women than on young men to be thin. Also, since anorexia is thought of mainly as a woman's problem, men may be less comfortable asking for help, leading them to be underrepresented in the statistics.

Because not all people with an eating disorder seek help, no one is sure exactly how many people suffer from anorexia. But the U.S. National Library of Medicine indicated in 2004 that it's estimated that 1 to 2 out of every 100 women have struggled with anorexia at some time in their lives. The National Association of Anorexia Nervosa and Associated Disorders (ANAD) reported that young women with anorexia are twelve times more likely to die than women who don't have anorexia—the highest death rate of any emotional problem. Anorexia is much less common in boys and men than in girls and women.

People who feel that they have little control over their lives are at a higher risk of developing anorexia. While other aspects of their lives may be overwhelming, the food they eat seems like the one thing they can control.

People are more likely to become anorexic if they tend to have very low self-esteem or are high achievers. Many people use anorexia as a way to gain more control over their lives. If a teen feels that her parents or teachers get to make all of her decisions for her, she may start to restrict the amount of food she eats to gain control at least over that part of her life.

The Definition of Anorexia

Doctors and psychiatrists rely on the *Diagnostic and Statistical Manual of Mental Disorders* (frequently known as the *DSM*) for the definitions they use in diagnosing conditions. The fifth edition of the *DSM*, which came out in 2013, lists three criteria for a diagnosis of anorexia. The patient must:

- Restrict the amount of food consumed
- Have an intense fear of gaining weight, despite being underweight
- Have a distorted idea of what he or she looks like, have his or her self-esteem be too closely tied to body shape or weight, or refuse to accept the serious health risks he or she is in.

Anorexia's Effects on the Body

Anorexia can have a big effect on your body and mind. If you have anorexia, you are afraid of gaining weight, so you restrict, or limit, the amount of food you consume. The result is weight loss. At first, the drop in weight may not be noticeable or look unhealthy. But in a short time, the weight loss becomes dramatic and threatens your health.

Anorexia affects all of your body functions. As the disorder progresses, your digestion slows down and you become constipated. Later, during the progression, you're always cold because you've lost the protective layer of fat that insulates you. Fine hair, called lanugo, grows all over your body. If you're female, your menstrual period stops. You also will look and feel tired and weak, have a pasty complexion, lose your hair, and have fainting spells and headaches. The soles of your palms and feet turn yellow because your body is lacking many of the nutrients it needs to function properly. Some of these side effects may not occur until severe weight loss has occurred.

An Eating Disorder 15

This young woman from England is suffering from an advanced case of anorexia. As you can see, her bones are visible through her skin and she has very little muscle. People with anorexia feel cold, tired, and weak much of the time.

When you aren't getting enough nutrition from food, your body will start to break down muscles in order to produce energy. Your liver and kidneys are damaged from this stress, leading to kidney failure. This can be fatal, or require you to be on dialysis for the rest of your life.

Anorexia may make women infertile, or unable to have children, because fertility depends on having a certain amount of body fat.

You may also develop osteoporosis—a condition in which your bones become brittle and may even break. Low bone mineral density in adolescent women who suffer from anorexia is a common problem, partly because of low calcium intake. Even young women who take calcium in their food or in supplements can get osteoporosis because amenorrhea—the absence of menstruation—can prevent their bodies from absorbing the calcium completely.

The heart can be especially affected. Anorexia disturbs the mineral balance in the body, which can cause cardiac arrest and death.

Anorexia's Effects on the Emotions

Anorexia often begins because of emotional reasons. People who suffer from eating disorders are trying to use food as a way to fill emotional needs—such as love and belonging, to ease loneliness, or to avoid difficult feelings and/or memories.

Yet anorexia actually worsens a painful emotional cycle. You become stressed out when you're around food because you feel tempted to eat. And if you do eat, you feel defeat and regret—you may even hate yourself. These feelings become so overwhelming, it's common for depression to set in.

Anorexia makes it hard for you to think and perceive things normally. When your body isn't getting the nutrients it needs, you run on adrenaline (a hormone that kicks in when you're fearful or stressed) instead of on energy from food. These chemical changes affect your personality. For example, you might have wider mood swings and a quicker temper.

Also, the more weight you lose, the more distorted your body image becomes. You see fat on your body when you really are dangerously thin. Thought distortion occurs because of the lack of nutrients. You also might not be able to concentrate.

MYTHS and FACTS

MYTH Anorexia is a lifestyle choice.

 Anorexia is a disease. It is not a lifestyle choice, and claims that it is one are very damaging to people suffering from or at risk of developing the disease.

MYTH Only young, white women suffer from anorexia.

 People of all ages, genders, and races can get anorexia.

MYTH All body changes that result from anorexia are reversible.

 Anorexia can damage organs such as the heart, liver, and kidneys permanently.

MYTH While restricting what you eat is bad, you can never exercise too much.

 Compulsive exercise—an unhealthy drive to overexercise in order to burn calories and stay thin—puts stress on your organs and joints, causing stress fractures and torn muscles.

MYTH Once a person with anorexia is back to a healthy weight, he or she is cured.

 Recovery is an ongoing process. Reaching—and even maintaining—a healthy weight is just part of the picture.

The Roots of Anorexia

People like having simple explanations for why things happen. However, there are plenty of things in life for which there is no single, simple explanation. Eating disorders such as anorexia are one of these things. You can't pin a person's eating disorder on any single thing. Eating disorders have complex, tangled roots.

Stress and Emotions

The amount of stress in a person's life can play a big role in the onset of anorexia. Anorexia is more likely to set in during a time of crisis or transition, such as reaching puberty, going to a new school, breaking up with someone, or having family problems. There are many other factors that help set the stage for anorexia, too. It's important to know as much as you can about how eating disorders take hold so you can keep yourself from falling into dangerous patterns.

Anorexia also has a lot to do with your emotions. Often, it sets in when you can't put your feelings into words or openly handle what's bothering you. With anorexia, losing weight becomes an obsession—a very intense, persistent thought that you can't block out. You may be very afraid that you are fat or are getting fat. At the same time, you may want to stifle these feelings. This leads to an increased desire for control over your emotions and actions.

Trying to Take Control

Often, people with anorexia will view not eating as a solution to problems, vowing to lose another 5 pounds (2.3 kg) when they feel upset or stressed out. They try to control their bodies by denying food when they can't control what is happening around them.

This is especially true if many things in your life feel beyond your control. If you aren't allowed to make decisions for yourself or have suffered physical, verbal, or sexual abuse, you may turn to dieting and exercise as ways to find control in your life.

Using anorexia to take control quickly becomes self-destructive. As anorexia sets in, it starts to control you. Soon all of your thoughts and actions revolve around food and eating rather than the emotions you are feeling.

If you feel out of control in your life, it is important to ask for help. Sometimes that just means telling people how you feel. For example, if your parents make family decisions without asking your opinion, you can tell them that you want to be more involved. Then you can work on a plan to keep you in the decision-making loop.

However, if you are in an abusive situation, you need to take strong action. Tell an adult you trust

Refusing to eat can give you a feeling of control over your own life. However, it is not a healthy choice.

that you need help. A teacher, guidance counselor, relative, or the parent of a friend can help you find a way to be safe.

Psychological Factors

There are several psychological factors that can contribute to anorexia. Scientists have noticed a correlation between eating disorders and anxiety disorders. A study published in the *American Journal of Psychiatry* in 2004 found that about two-thirds of people with eating disorders had wrestled with an anxiety disorder at some

Several different studies have found that teens who are struggling with depression or anxiety disorders are more likely to develop anorexia.

point in their lives. The most common of anxiety diseases they dealt with were obsessive-compulsive disorder (also known as OCD) and social phobia.

There's also a close tie between eating disorders and depression. For example, 21 percent of the bipolar patients in a 2008 study by researchers at the University of Pittsburgh Medical Center could be diagnosed as having an eating disorder at some point in their lives. Other studies have shown that patients suffering from both depression and an eating disorder are less likely to have a relapse after treatment for the eating disorder if they also receive treatment—in the form of either medications or cognitive behavioral therapy—for depression.

Body Chemicals

People with eating disorders often have imbalances of hormones and other chemicals in their body. Not eating enough of the right foods could cause these imbalances, but it's also possible that the chemicals themselves help trigger the eating disorder if other factors are there or if the environmental background sets the stage for it.

People with anorexia tend to have high levels of the hormone cortisol, which gets the body ready to react to a stressful situation. Part of this hormone's job is to inhibit a chemical called neuropeptide Y, which stimulates appetite. Scientists think cortisol might help explain why people with anorexia respond to stressful situations by limiting their food.

The brain chemical serotonin may also have something to do with anorexia. This chemical gives you a feeling of well-being and affects your appetite. Researchers have found that people with anorexia have different levels of serotonin than people who don't have anorexia. They have found that people who become anorexic have too much serotonin, then they starve themselves, which lowers the serotonin, but then the brain adapts to the change by adding more serotonin to the body. It becomes a vicious circle because the little bit of serotonin sets off the brain receptors, and the receptors keep trying to adjust.

Genetic Factors

Although anorexia is usually thought to be related to emotions and social pressures, doctors have now come to understand that some people have genes (traits inherited from your mother and father) that predispose them to having anorexia. Some researchers believe that certain inherited neurotic symptoms, such as anxiety or depression, may account for at least part of this risk. A study that was published in *The Journal of Clinical Investigation* in 2013 linked two genetic mutations—ESRRA and HDAC4—to a predisposition to developing eating disorders. Other studies have linked eating disorders to the genes that control serotonin (a neurotransmitter, or chemical that relays information in the nervous system), norepinephrine (a stress hormone), and estrogen (a compound involved in the female reproductive system).

Because of this genetic link, anorexia tends to run in families. A study by scientist Cynthia Bulik of the University of North Carolina Eating Disorders Program found that genetic factors accounted for more than half of all anorexia cases among a group of 31,000 Swedish twins. If your sister or mother has anorexia, you have a higher than average likelihood of developing it, too. But even if you have a genetic risk of developing the disorder or a family history, it doesn't mean you will definitely get anorexia. Scientists agree that, though there is a major genetic component to the disease, environmental factors also play a role.

The Roots of Anorexia

There are many traits you can inherit from your parents. Unfortunately a predisposition toward anorexia is one of them. This does not mean you will necessarily develop the disease, just that you are at higher risk of doing so.

Social Factors

Our society places a high value on thinness. In fact, many people believe that in order to be beautiful, you have to be thin. When the media—television, movies, and advertising—widely promote this ideal, it becomes difficult to ignore. And it affects what you think is normal. You may start to think that all people are supposed to look as thin as actors and models, when in fact very few people in the world are that thin.

This ideal also affects your feelings about yourself. You may think that losing weight will make you feel more beautiful, loved, accepted, or popular. But trying to be that thin is unhealthy and impossible for most people.

Changing Ideas of Beauty

Even though thin is in now, that wasn't always the case. From thousands of years ago up to the mid-1960s, the ideal woman was shapely and soft. Women with full figures were considered desirable because they represented fertility, sexuality, and wealth.

You can see this ideal in the art of many societies. Often, goddesses were portrayed with curvy breasts, stomachs, and buttocks. You also can see this ideal of the female body in the Renaissance paintings of Peter Paul Rubens (this is why full-figured women sometimes are called Rubenesque).

This ideal of the female body held true for a long time. But somewhere along the way, ideas changed. And they have had dramatic effects on American society even very recently. The thin ideal went to the extreme by the end of the twentieth century. In the 1990s, the "heroin chic" look (characterized by a pale complexion and a drug-addict/wasted-away appearance) became popular. Models in

Many of today's stars (like Keira Knightley, seen here) are very slender. Fans often aspire to be movie-star thin, but, depending on their body types, the look may not be healthy for them.

the fashion industry (both male and female) with very thin bodies and dark circles under their eyes became the ultimate statement of what was cool and sexy.

Although the "heroin chic" look has mainly gone out of fashion, thin is definitely still in, and the thinner the better. Hosts on the red carpet at the Academy Awards ceremony praise actresses for looking especially skinny. Celebrities brag about how quickly they were able to get back into their "size 0 jeans" after having a baby. You may hear those messages and feel like you have to be that thin yourself.

The Problem with Thin Being In

Placing too much value on thinness has had negative consequences, especially for teenage girls. It can lead you to become anti-fat—cutting all fat out of your diet and trying to eliminate it from your body. And that can lead to unhealthy dieting and anorexia, which interrupt how you're supposed to grow. People need to eat healthy foods to take care of their bodies. And as a teen, you need to eat even more than other people because your body is still growing and changing.

Another problem with wanting to be thin is that most people are not naturally thin. All bodies look different and grow at different rates. Genes play a major role in deciding what body shape you will have, just as they determine the color of your hair and your eyes.

If you have set an unrealistic goal about how you want to look, you will feel disappointed when you cannot attain it. This can cause the depression that contributes to the onset of eating disorders.

Friends and Family

Having friends is important. You want to fit in and be accepted. But fitting in can mean feeling pressure to dress, look, and act in a way that reinforces the problems that lead to eating disorders. Many people—girls especially—will bond through "fat talk," or sympathizing over how fat they think they look and how much they hate their bodies. As a group, you may be bringing each other down.

Like your friends, family members may indulge in fat talk. It isn't uncommon for parents and kids to go on diets together—even when the son or daughter hasn't hit puberty yet. Sometimes parents may directly criticize you for what you look like or how much you eat. This may be intended as concern for your social life and goals—"If you keep eating desserts every night, you'll never find a

Parents who are critical of their children can be a contributing factor to anorexia. Parents who are critical of their children's weight or appearance can have a particularly damaging effect.

prom date." But it does more harm than good. The message comes across that you're not good enough the way you are.

These kinds of negative comments can set up a battlefield mentality between you and your parents. By commenting on your food intake, your parents come across as criticizing—even controlling—you. And you may respond by defying them. You may purposely overeat in order to enrage your thin-conscious parents. Or you could fall into anorexic patterns, thinking that being thinner will bring approval or that starvation will bring attention. But these are unhealthy ways to cope with the problem.

Does your mom constantly complain that she's too fat? Is your older brother always on a diet? Having family members who are obsessed with their weight could rub off on you. It's not only the urge to diet that tends to run in families. Your sister may be a gymnast and practice five hours every day. Your father might be a workaholic who spends eighty hours per week in the office. Perfectionism and other compulsions are traits that can make it easier for you to develop anorexia. These traits could be in your family's genes, or you could develop them from watching your family.

It's possible to speak up against the anti-fat mentality. When you want to be accepted by others, it may be hard to believe that weight does not matter. But there are things that matter more—like finding out who you are inside, setting and meeting goals, and tapping into the energy inside of you. If people around you make a big deal about weight, you don't have to go along with it.

Your attitudes about yourself can bring on or prevent an eating disorder. By improving your self-esteem, you can take a giant step toward preventing anorexia.

Combatting Risk Factors

While there are plenty of risk factors for anorexia, it's important to remember that not everyone who has risk factors develops anorexia. Even if several of these risk factors apply to you, it doesn't mean that you automatically will develop an eating disorder. In fact, being aware that you are at risk may help you stop a potential eating problem before it starts.

Your Self-Esteem

People with high self-esteem—a positive view of themselves—have a lower risk of developing an eating disorder. High self-esteem leads people to value their own ideas and opinions, be eager to try new things, and speak up when something is bothering them.

In comparison, people at risk for anorexia tend to have a less-than-flattering attitude about themselves. They feel misunderstood, think their ideas aren't important, try very hard to be perfect, and may shy away from trying new things because they're afraid to fail. If you have low self-esteem, you probably feel that you have little control over what happens to you. There are other attitudes that make you vulnerable to anorexia, too.

Low self-esteem leads people to minimize their accomplishments. This means you don't credit yourself where credit is due. If you score the winning point in a basketball game, you say, "Well,

Many factors, including how you are treated by your family, your friends, your peers, and the authority figures in your life, can impact your self-esteem.

anyone could have done it." If you ace a test, you say, "It wasn't that hard anyway." Low self-esteem also leads people to write off the positive things other people say about them. They might think, "Well, she's my mom. Of course she thinks I'm great!" or "He doesn't know what he's talking about."

When the unhappiness and tension that you feel gets directed toward your body, that is a sign of an eating disorder. So is thinking that losing weight will make you feel better about yourself and will make other people like you. If you start feeling this way, don't keep it inside. Talk to a trusted adult about it.

It's also a good idea to try to do things to build up your self-esteem. Make a list of things that you are good at or accomplishments that you are proud of. Spend more time doing things that you enjoy and with people you care about. Avoid people or situations that make you feel bad about yourself.

Weight and Dieting

Have you ever gone on a diet and lost a few pounds? If you have, you probably have heard comments from your friends and family such as, "Wow, you look great! Did you lose weight?" But gain a few pounds, and you may hear just the opposite. Knowing that your weight gain has been noticed and made fun of can really hurt your feelings.

Our society values thin, toned bodies. So when someone loses weight, they generally get praised for it, even if they weren't overweight to begin with. Getting cheered on in your weight loss can give you the urge to lose even more weight than you need to lose.

Gaining weight can lead to hurtful or insulting comments from others. It can also make you feel uncomfortable in your own body. Your body doesn't look exactly the same as it used to look. Maybe your favorite bikini doesn't fit anymore, or you don't look quite as good in your jeans.

If you are worried that you might be overweight, talk to your doctor about it. If he or she says that you need to lose some weight, come up with a plan to eat more healthily and exercise more often. However, if your doctor says you are at a healthy weight, stick to the routines you have. Do your best to ignore the pressure from those around you to be super-skinny.

Difficult Times

Life is full of uncertainty and change. A move to a new town, parents divorcing, or the death of a family member can all cause major

Problems with friends, whether that means a falling out with an old friend group or trouble making friends in a new school, can be stressful. Anorexia is an unhealthy response to this stress.

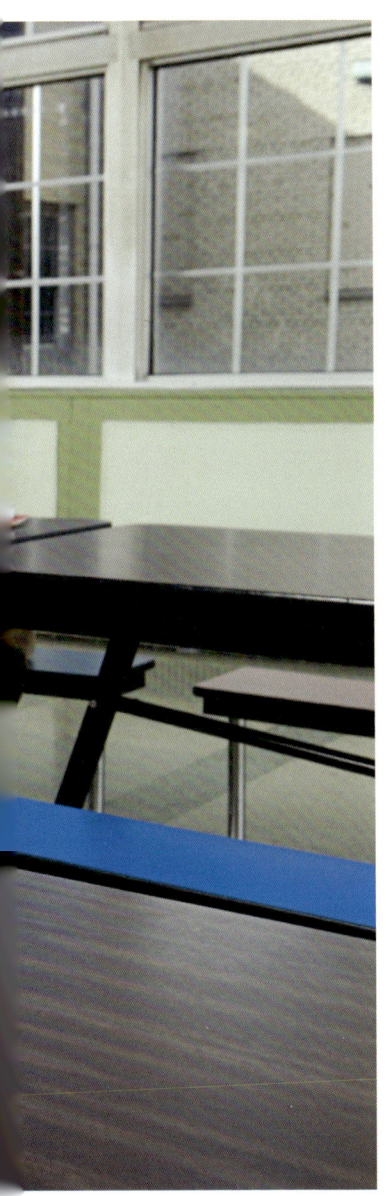

upheavals. These changes can be very emotional and stressful. They can make you feel like you have no control over your own life. People sometimes respond to stressful situations by trying to reign in the things they can control—such as the food they eat.

If you are going through a difficult period in your life, be aware that you are at a greater risk of developing an eating disorder. Pay attention to your own habits. If you feel like you want more control over your life, think about healthy ways to make this happen. Make a list of the things that frustrate you and think about which ones you can change—as well as which ones you can't. Figure out which people in your life really respect you for who you are, and spend more time with those people.

Sports

The aim in sports is to win. You need to run the fastest, swim the hardest, and score the most goals in order to be the best. With these high expectations, it's no wonder that athletes are at higher risk for eating disorders than other people.

Sports are physically demanding, and people who participate in them need to be in good shape. Some athletes take their quest to be thin too far, though. They think that if they lose more weight, they'll be faster and more agile.

Some sports, like wrestling, actually require that athletes stay within a certain weight range. Others, like figure skating and dancing, press the idea that only thin, lithe bodies look good enough to be on the stage and ice. Parents and coaches can make young athletes even more prone to eating disorders by pushing them to lose weight in order to perform better.

Being Proactive

Stay in touch with your feelings and what's going on in your life. Express yourself, and don't be afraid to ask for help when you need it. You can use your self-knowledge to keep from falling into the patterns that lead to a full-blown eating disorder. This can mean finding friends who don't make a big deal out of food and body size. Writing down your thoughts—in a journal, blog, or any other format—can be helpful. Getting involved with sports, hobbies, or youth groups is also a good idea. Find an adult you trust (family member, doctor, or counselor), and go to them for help when you start feeling out of control. Always remember that you are not alone. There is help available when and if you need it.

Don't go along with fat talk. If your friends are in the habit of putting themselves down and criticizing their bodies, let them know that it bugs you. Be positive. Try saying, "Actually, I like myself. I look just like my aunt did at my age, and I think she's so cool. So what if I'm not a size 2."

Ask your doctor what weight is healthiest for your body. When you see a model in a magazine who is 5'7" and weighs 110 pounds (49.9 kg), you won't have to compare yourself—you'll be able to set your own weight goals.

Know what you're up against. Go to your local library, search the Internet, and talk to your doctor about eating disorders. Know

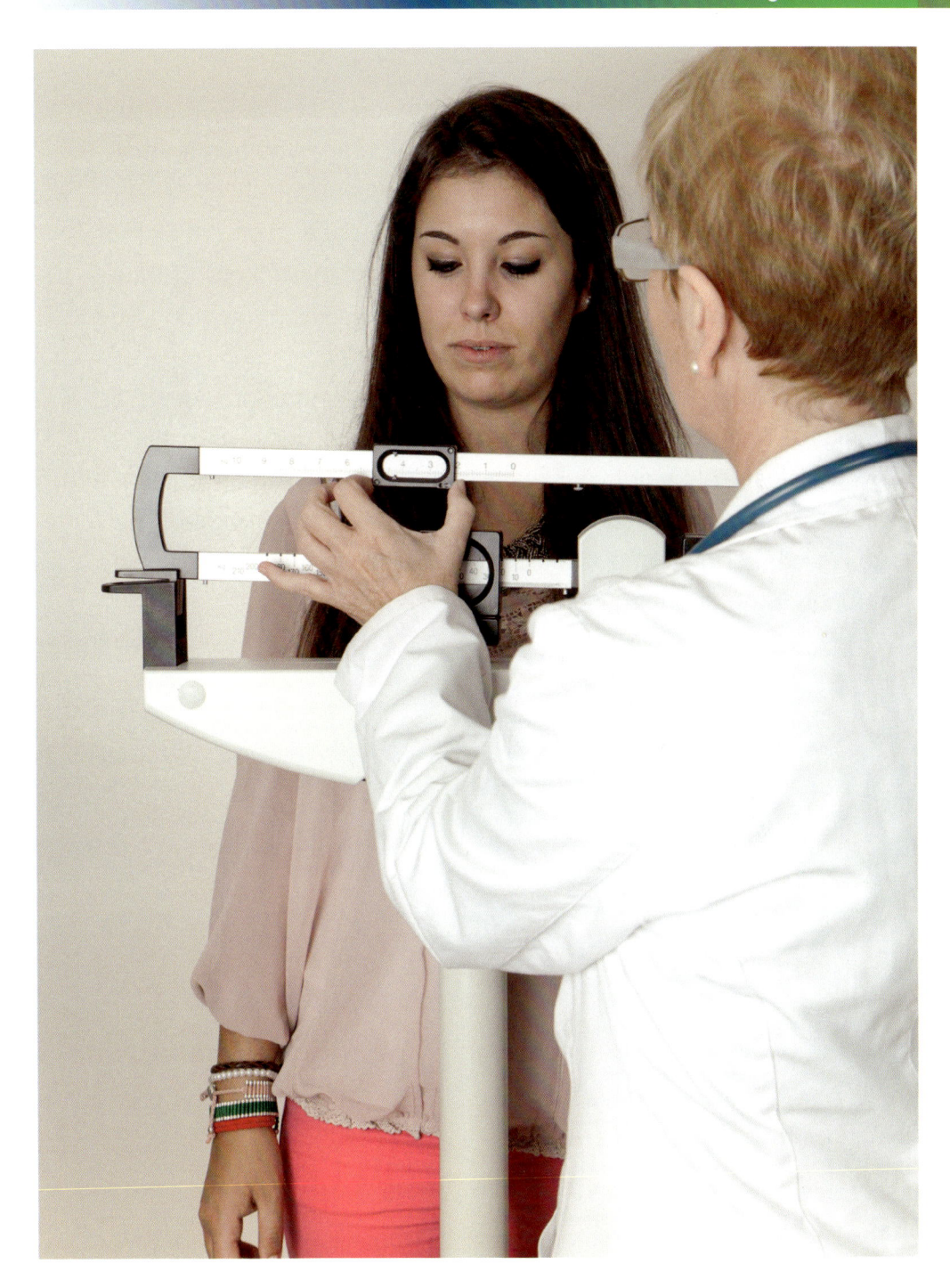

Your ideal weight should be determined by what your doctor says, not by what your friends or classmates say or by the images you see in the media.

how they start and what they can do to you. Stay away from any sites that promote anorexia. They can encourage you to start making dangerous choices about your health.

Think critically about the advertising you see. If you're sick of magazines showing only waiflike models, let the editors of those magazines know. You can pressure them by saying you won't buy their publications anymore.

Get involved with sports that emphasize strength (such as basketball and biking) rather than body shape (such as ballet or gymnastics). Throw out your scale, and give away clothes that don't fit. Save up some money to buy clothes that feel comfortable. When you're comfortable and relaxed, your fabulous inner self will shine through. Stop counting calories.

Symptoms of Anorexia

It's easy to recognize when a person is in the late stages of anorexia. She or he will be obviously underweight, with visible bones, brittle hair, and dry skin. However, it can be harder to spot someone who is in the early stages of anorexia. Early on, the cues that somebody is suffering from anorexia are more likely to be in that person's behavior than in his or her appearance.

How Anorexia Starts

As you know, anorexia often starts as a diet. But the more weight you lose, the more you want to lose. In the beginning, you may even receive admiration and praise as you start to lose weight. The attention feels good. But privately, you feel that you still need to lose more weight.

Extreme Dieting

One of the first signs of anorexia is that you make your diet regimen more and more strict. This means making what seem to be sensible choices at first—cutting out all red meat, skipping dessert, and choosing low-fat or nonfat alternatives to foods such as cream

Salad is a healthy food, but that doesn't mean it is healthy to eat only simple salads. To get all the nutrients that your body needs, you should eat a mix of foods.

cheese and salad dressing. You soon begin restricting your intake of other foods, too. You may limit yourself to white meat and vegetables and reduce the size of your portions. Eventually your diet may become so extreme that you're hardly eating anything.

A Warped View of Yourself

Soon shedding pounds becomes the most important thing in your life—the yardstick by which you measure and judge yourself. You may start checking yourself in the mirror and weighing yourself several times each day. Your moods are deeply affected by what you see. You're relieved if the scale shows weight loss and devastated if it shows a gain.

Other aspects of your self-perception have changed, too. When you look at your body, you see yourself more as a set of body parts—hips, thighs, stomach—than as a whole person. You become rigid in your thinking, vowing to eliminate pounds in the areas you don't like on your body. You think of losing weight as a positive action, not realizing that this intense scrutiny is actually harming your self-esteem.

Rituals

Rituals are an important ingredient in the development of anorexia. Often, rituals center around mealtimes. You may devise a rigid plan in which you eat different foods, cut the food up into tiny pieces, and chew a certain number of times before you swallow.

It's also common to inspect your food intensely, checking for anything that looks funny. If you find something you can't identify, you feel that it's okay to reject the meal.

How Anorexia Changes You

As you continue to deny yourself food, your body will begin to change. At first, the changes may not be noticeable to you or people around you. But eventually, the weight loss will have dramatic effects on your looks and physical health.

As you get deeper and deeper into your self-denying rituals, your normal self shuts down even more. Being hungry all the time alters your personality. To a healthy person, your actions will appear more and more irrational.

Your Body

When you have full-blown anorexia, your body is likely to change in several ways. Muscle weakness is common, along with dizziness or fainting. You're likely to have trouble sleeping and to always feel cold. Constipation, bloating, dehydration, and poor circulation all become issues. You will be tired much of the time, but may have periods of hyperactivity as well. Skin problems—such as dry skin or yellow palms and soles—develop. Your teeth may start decaying. While you are likely to find the hair on your head falling out, you will probably grow a coat of fine, downy hair (called lanugo) on your body. If you're a woman who has started menstruating, you are likely to experience irregular or absent menstrual periods. These symptoms are all signs that something is seriously wrong with your body.

Your Personality

One typical change in behavior is that you grow more impatient with others. You become more focused on yourself. You withdraw from friends and family by not going out or returning phone calls. People around you may express serious concern about your extreme weight loss, but you're convinced that they are trying to sabotage you. You feel that the anorexia gives you a sense of power and invincibility.

Although you still believe that the anorexia is making you powerful and in control, you probably feel scared and lonely underneath. This loneliness may become worse as the illness progresses. You may get into more fights with your family or, even worse, watch family members fight about (or over) you.

Anorexia causes changes in both your mind and your body. These changes get more pronounced as the disease becomes more advanced.

People may start to relate to you differently, alternately babying, arguing with, and avoiding you. You may end up feeling more alienated than you did at the start.

Confronting a Person with Anorexia

One of the hardest things you can do is confront someone you think is suffering from anorexia. If you suspect that someone you care

When talking to a friend about his or her eating disorder, it is important to be supportive rather than confrontational. Don't make your friend feel shame, guilt, or blame.

about has anorexia, start by educating yourself about the problem. Read up on eating disorders, and talk to a therapist or counselor for information.

Find a quiet time that's good to talk. Don't confront someone when other people are around and an argument could start. Listen to what the person has to say. Hold back comments about yourself and your own problems for the time being. Use "I" statements instead of "you" statements. Rather than accusing, let the person know gently that her illness is noticeable and has affected you. For example: "I noticed you haven't been eating. Is something wrong?" This opens up a dialogue more effectively than simply saying, "You look sick."

Understand that your help may not be taken. It's important to let the person know that you care about her, but if she isn't ready to change, you can't force her. With that in mind, let your friend know that you are available if she needs to reach out to you in the future.

10 GREAT QUESIONS TO ASK YOURSELF ABOUT ANOREXIA

1. What does my doctor say about my weight?

2. Does my weight play a big role in determining my self-worth?

3. Am I afraid of being fat?

4. Do friends and family members suggest that I am too skinny?

5. Do I believe I am fat, even if others say I am underweight?

6. Do I ever lie by saying I have already eaten a meal when I really haven't?

7. Do I set strict limits for the number of calories I let myself eat each day?

8. Do I fast, skipping meals or going without food for one or more days?

9. Do I limit the amount of food my body absorbs by vomiting or using laxatives?

10. Do I spend a lot of time thinking about food, including coming up with ways to avoid eating?

The Recovery Process

For a person to recover from anorexia, that person needs to acknowledge that she has a problem and genuinely want to get better. While getting sick may not be a conscious choice, getting better almost always is. You can choose to starve yourself to the point where you become sick and controlled by your disease, or you can choose to become healthy.

Understanding What Is at Stake

If the anorexia continues, you may risk death. Your organs will start to shut down, and you will have liver, kidney, and heart problems. But it's possible to stop the illness before then. At first, you may not want to stop. Or, you may want to but are afraid to do so. It is scary, but that's part of the illness of anorexia. It makes you feel as if it's the only thing that matters. It makes you fear that if you give up anorexia, you'll be nothing without it. It becomes a part of your identity, which makes giving it up seem like losing a part of yourself. But the truth is, anorexia is holding you back. It takes up all of your energy—energy you otherwise could spend growing and learning about yourself and living a healthy life.

It is possible to recover with the help of your parents, friends, and doctors. Once you break the pattern, you'll see how quickly new opportunities open to you. Admitting you have an eating disorder

If denying your eating disorder caused conflict with your parents in the past, it can be hard to bring the topic up again once you are ready to talk about it. Even if that talk is difficult, though, it will be worth having.

is the hardest thing you can do when you have anorexia. People probably have tried to confront you about it before. But sometimes people's concerns can feel like pressures and threats. Parents may say, "You're tearing this family apart," or "Your father and I don't know what to do with you," or "If you don't eat something, I'm sending you to a therapist."

You probably want—and need—people's love and concern. It's possible that someone may confront you when the time is right and you're ready to take him or her up on an offer for help. But, especially if you're taken by surprise or someone doesn't express himself or herself in the best way, you're likely to reject any help that is offered.

That's why it's important to take matters into your own hands and choose whom to tell and how to say it. The first time you admit to another person that you have a problem can feel very awkward. But if you think it through first, you'll feel more comfortable when the time comes.

Getting Help

Tell an authority figure. You can tell a friend, too, but it's important to tell someone who is likely to have more insight about what to do. This could be your parents or a friend's parents, an grandparent, an aunt or uncle, a teacher, a counselor, or someone from your religious organization.

Pick a time that's good to talk. Make sure you will have a quiet place and enough time to really discuss the matter in depth. Schedule your meeting in advance, even if it will be a family meeting. Bring a support person with you if you need it. This could be a friend or a professional, such as a social worker or therapist, who already knows that you have an eating disorder.

Think about what you're going to say. You don't have to write down a script, but it may help to come up with a few key phrases or points beforehand, such as:

- "I know you have brought this up with me before and I denied it. But I have a problem with food. I'm ready to talk about it now."
- "I haven't been eating. I need your help."
- "I need to bring a problem out into the open. I'm afraid of eating. I need to talk with you about what to do."

Know that people's reactions may not be what you expected. Although you planned in advance, you may find that the person isn't comfortable handling the information. It may mean that someone gets angry at you, tries to one-up you with a story about herself, or goes on as if nothing has happened. If this happens, you will need to speak to another person who can help you.

Consulting a Doctor

A good first step if you think you might have anorexia is to visit your primary-care doctor. Even if you haven't been to the doctor in a while, it's important that she knows what's going on. Your doctor will examine you to see how your eating disorder has affected your health. Often your primary-care physician may refer you to an eating disorder specialist.

First, the doctor will check your overall health: your height and weight, heart rate, blood pressure, temperature, and heartbeat. She will also look for other signs of anorexia, such as brittle nails or dry skin. She may give you tests that check your heart, chemicals in your blood, and the function of your liver, kidneys, and thyroid gland. Some of these tests will help the doctor know whether your problem is an eating disorder or another health problem. Then your doctor will probably ask you a few questions, such as:

- How have you been eating?
- How has your weight changed recently?
- What are you doing to lose weight?
- Are you having problems with your family or friends?

A Recovery Plan

To get better, you'll probably need several kinds of treatments. The treatments can focus on your body and your mind.

It's important to be involved in deciding what your recovery plan will be. Sit down with your primary-care doctor and family and talk about the options that are available. Together, you can decide what works best for you, depending on your needs and your family's financial situation.

Healing Your Body

The first goal in your therapy is to get your body healthy. It's possible that if you are very ill, you may need to be hospitalized. The doctors there will monitor your heart and other vital signs. They'll make sure that you have the right balance of fluids and chemicals in your body.

Because experts have found a connection between eating disorders and depression, antidepressants such as Prozac have been used to treat eating disorders. If you are given a prescription, ask your doctor and therapist about the drug and its side effects. You have the right to request a change in your medication if you feel it is not working.

Once you're healthy enough to go home, you may see a dietician who specializes in eating disorders. This person can help you plan out your meals to make sure you get enough calories and can help you develop better eating habits.

Treating Your Mind

One major part of recovery from anorexia is psychotherapy, or therapy for short. This is not as scary as it sounds. Basically, therapy is talking to a neutral person (a therapist) about what's going on in your life. The more you talk, the more you discover about yourself. Therapy is especially helpful for dealing with eating disorders. The better you know yourself, the better equipped you are to build your self-esteem. At the same time, you can work on pinpointing the patterns of thought or the life experiences that brought on the eating disorder and prevent them from happening again.

Some people recovering from anorexia find talking difficult. The feeling that one has no voice or needs to hide one's voice is sometimes a contributing factor to the development of anorexia. People recovering from anorexia sometimes prefer to express their thoughts, opinions, and feelings in nonverbal ways. Music, graphic art, and drama therapies have proven to be very helpful in the recovery process. In music therapy, people might participate in structured groups in which they write songs, beat a drum, and sing karaoke. These approaches can help patients overcome a lack of self-esteem, a fear of rejection, and poor communication skills.

You may find that a clinic situation works best for you. Clinics specializing in eating disorders are often free. They may be inpatient,

Talking to a therapist one-on-one, as this young woman is doing, can play an important part in your recovery from anorexia. However, every patient needs to find the form of therapy to which she or he is best suited.

which means you live there while receiving treatment, or outpatient, which means you come in during the day and go home at night. The following are just a few of the different kinds of therapy you might try:

- Individual therapy: You meet with a therapist one-on-one. A therapist may be a psychologist (a therapist with a Ph.D. degree), a psychiatrist (a psychologist who is also a medical doctor), a

CONQUERING ANOREXIA

Recovering from anorexia is a life-long process. That said, people who have suffered from the disease in the past can still live full and happy lives.

licensed professional counselor (LPC), a psychotherapist, or a licensed social worker.
- Family therapy: You and your family meet with a therapist. This helps your family learn more about eating disorders and how to help you.
- Group therapy: You meet with a group of people who share the same type of problem you are grappling with and, together with a therapist, discuss solutions.
- Self-help: You meet with other people who are recovering from eating disorders to share insights. Unlike other avenues to recovery, self-help is not led by a therapist. Members of a group form networks with each other.

A Successful Recovery

No matter what kind of therapy you choose, it's important to stay involved in the decision-making process. You may find that your treatment plan isn't working right for you. Or, you may want to throw out the plan and go back to anorexic patterns. Don't give up! You already have made the choice for health.

If you do find yourself sliding back into bad old habits, though, don't despair. Recovery is a challenging, ongoing process, and lots of people have moments of backsliding. When you notice anorexic habits or thoughts returning, speak to someone—preferably your therapist, doctor, or group therapy members—about it. Remember how far you have already come.

There are many routes toward recovery. If you can speak up about how you feel, you can work together with others to decide what to do. There are many different approaches for treating anorexia. Sometimes it takes time before you find the right one. Recovery from anorexia is one of the hardest things you will ever do—but it's worth it.

GLOSSARY

ADRENALINE A hormone that kicks in when a person is fearful or stressed.

AMENORRHEA The absence of menstruation, or getting your period regularly.

APPETITE SUPPRESSANT A drug or chemical that reduces hunger/appetite and keeps you from wanting as much food.

BINGE To eat large amounts of food in one sitting.

BODY IMAGE The way you perceive your body and how you think others perceive your body.

BULIMIA An eating disorder in which someone eats a lot and then purges the food.

CARDIAC ARREST When your heart stops beating.

CIRCULATION The movement of blood though the body due to the pumping of the heart.

CONSTIPATION Difficulty having bowel movements.

CORTISOL A hormone that gets your body ready to deal with stressful situations.

DIAGNOSIS Identifying a disease by recognizing its symptoms, or signs.

DIURETIC A drug that causes an increase in the amount of urine the kidneys produce.

GENES The basic units of heredity.

HYPERACTIVITY Being constantly active and full of energy.

INFERTILITY The inability to have children.

LAXATIVE A drug or substance that brings on a bowel movement.

NUTRITION Eating a healthy selection of foods in the amounts necessary to maintain health.

OSTEOPOROSIS A condition that causes bones to become brittle and fragile.

PREDISPOSITION A tendency toward something.

PURGE To rid the body of food, usually through vomiting, exercise, or laxatives.

RITUAL A set way of performing certain actions.

SEROTONIN A chemical in the brain that gives you a feeling of well-being and affects your appetite.

SYMPTOM Something that is considered a sign of a disease.

ULCERS Tears or holes in the lining of the stomach, throat, or mouth.

VITAL SIGNS Measurements of the body's most important functions, such as body temperature and heart rate.

FOR MORE INFORMATION

Eating Disorders Coalition
P.O. Box 96503-98807
Washington, DC 20090
(202) 543-9570
http://www.eatingdisorderscoalition.org

This national organization advocates for patients with eating disorders. It pushes for eating disorders to be considered a public health priority and to ensure insurance coverage for their treatment. Among other things, the group holds conferences, has an ongoing letter writing campaign, and organizes lobbying days.

Families Empowered and Supporting Treatment of Eating Disorders
P.O. Box 11608
Milwaukee, WI 53211
(855) 503-3278
http://www.feast-ed.org

This international organization, often known by the acronym FEAST, exists to support people who are caregivers for eating disorder patients. It believes that families are key to a successful recovery. It was formed by a group of parents in 2003 and today has branches in the United States, Canada, Australia, and the United Kingdom.

National Alliance on Mental Illness
3803 N. Fairfax Drive, Suite 100
Arlington, VA 22203
(703) 524-7600
http://www.nami.org

This organization, often known by the acronym NAMI, was founded in 1979 to support the millions of Americans who suffer from mental illness. It is a good source of information about eating disorders, as well as other conditions—such as depression and anxiety disorders—that often go hand-in-hand with these disorders.

National Association of Anorexia Nervosa and Associated Disorders
750 E. Diehl Road, #127
Naperville, IL 60563
(630) 577-1333
http://www.anad.org
The National Association of Anorexia Nervosa and Associated Disorders, often known as ANAD, can help you find treatment. This nonprofit organization coordinates support groups for those struggling with eating disorders and has a helpline—the number is (630) 577-1330—for those looking for treatment.

National Eating Disorders Association
165 W. 46th Street, Suite 402
New York, NY 10036
(800) 931-2237
https://www.nationaleatingdisorders.org
The NEDA is the biggest nonprofit group working to prevent eating disorders in the United States. The organization formed in 2001, when two preexisting organizations—Eating Disorders Awareness & Prevention (EDAP) and the American Anorexia Bulimia Association (AABA)—merged. It aims to support both people with eating disorder and their families.

National Eating Disorder Information Centre
200 Elizabeth Street, ES 7-421
Toronto, ON M5G 2C4
Canada
(416) 340-4156
http://www.nedic.ca
NEDIC works to raise awareness about eating disorders and runs several outreach programs focused on prevention. It operates a toll-free helpline (1-866-NEDIC-20) with information about treatment for eating disorders, and its website has a lot of useful information, too.

Stanford Eating Disorders Research Program
Department of Child and Adolescent Psychiatry
401 Quarry Road
Stanford, CA 94305
(650) 498-4468
http://edresearch.stanford.edu
Both a research facility and a treatment center, this program hopes to both treat patients with eating disorders and study those patients to gain a better understanding of how eating disorders work. The program's eating disorders clinic offers both inpatient and outpatient care.

University of California, San Diego
Department of Psychiatry
Eating Disorders Center for Treatment and Research
4510 Executive Drive, Suite 315
San Diego, CA 92121
(858) 534-8019
http://eatingdisorders.ucsd.edu/index.shtml

This center at UCSD studies the biological aspects of eating disorders, with a particular emphasis on the neurobiology of anorexia and bulimia. The staff develops individual treatment plans for patients that draw on the latest scientific understanding of the diseases.

University of North Carolina Center of Excellence for Eating Disorders
Neurosciences Hospital
101 Manning Drive, CB #7160
Chapel Hill, NC 27599
(984) 974-3834
http://www.med.unc.edu/psych/eatingdisorders
This university medical program focuses on treating people with eating disorders, training health professionals to work with patients who suffer from those diseases, and research into the causes of the diseases. The center's website has links to studies that are recruiting and links to useful resources.

Websites:

Because of the changing nature of Internet links, Rosen Publishing has developed an online list of websites related to the subject of this book. This site is updated regularly. Please use this link to access the list:

http://www.rosenlinks.com/CED/Anor

FOR FURTHER READING

Anderson, Laurie Halse. *Wintergirls*. New York, NY: Viking Books for Young Readers, 2009.

Arnold, Carrie. *Decoding Anorexia: How Breakthroughs in Science Offer Hope for Eating Disorders*. New York, NY: Routledge, 2012.

Brown, Harriet. *Body of Truth: How Science, History, and Culture Drive Our Obsession with Weight—and What We Can Do about It*. Boston, MA: Da Capo Press, 2015.

Brown, Harriet. *Brave Girl Eating: A Family's Struggle with Anorexia*. New York, NY: William Morrow Paperbacks, 2011.

Bulik, Cynthia M. *The Woman in the Mirror: How to Stop Confusing What You Look Like with Who You Are*. New York, NY: Walker & Company, 2011.

Costin, Carolyn, and Gwen Schubert Grabb. *8 Keys to Recovery from an Eating Disorder: Effective Strategies from Therapeutic Practice and Personal Experience*. New York, NY: W. W. Norton & Company, 2011.

Dunkle, Elena, and Clare B. Dunkle. *Elena Vanishing: A Memoir*. San Francisco, CA: Chronicle Books, 2015.

Hopkins, Ellen. *Perfect*. New York, NY: Margaret K. McElderry Books, 2011.

Hornbacher, Marya. *Wasted: A Memoir of Anorexia and Bulimia*. Updated Edition. New York, NY: Harper Perennial, 2014.

Liu, Aimee. *Restoring Our Bodies, Reclaiming Our Lives: Guidance and Reflections on Recovery from Eating Disorders*. Boston, MA: Trumpeter Books, 2011.

Lock, James, and Daniel Le Grange. *Help Your Teenager Beat an Eating Disorder*. Second Edition. New York, NY: Guilford Press, 2015.

O'Connor, Richard A. *From Virtue to Vice: Negotiating Anorexia (Food, Nutrition, and Culture)*. New York, NY: Berghahn Books, 2015.

Osgood, Kelsey. *How to Disappear Completely: On Modern Anorexia*. New York, NY: The Overlook Press, 2013.

Poppink, Joanna. *Healing Your Hungry Heart: Recovering from Your Eating Disorder*. San Francisco, CA: Conari Press, 2011.

Shahan, Sherry. *Skin and Bones*. Park Ridge, IL: Albert Whitman & Company, 2014.

Taylor, Julia V. *The Body Image Workbook for Teens: Activities to Help Girls Develop a Healthy Body Image in an Image-Obsessed World*. Oakland, CA: Instant Help, 2014.

Thomas, Jennifer J., and Jenni Schaefer. *Almost Anorexic: Is My (or My Loved One's) Relationship with Food a Problem?* Center City, MN: Hazelden Publishing, 2013.

INDEX

A

abusive situations, 19–20
anorexia
  and anxiety disorder, 20–21, 22
  in athletes, 34
  causes, 16, 20, 21
  death rates, 7, 12
  defined, 14
  emotional effects, 16, 40–42
  and family pressure, 27–28
  genetic factors, 22
  in males and females, 12
  and need for control, 13, 18, 19, 41
  occurrence rates, 12
  physical effects, 14, 17, 40
  prevention, 34, 36
  recovery, 17, 45, 47–51, 53
  risk factors, 7, 13, 18, 20, 29–34
  social factors, 24, 26, 27–28
  symptoms, 37, 39–42
anxiety disorder, 20–21, 22

B

beauty ideals, 24, 26
binge eating disorder, 8, 10
bipolar disorder, 21
body image, 16, 39
bulimia, 8, 10

C

clinics, 50–51
cold, feeling, 14, 40
compulsive exercise, 17
confrontation, 42–43
constipation, 14, 40
cortisol hormone, 21

D

depression, 16, 21, 22, 26, 49–50
dialysis, 15
dietician, 50
dieting/weight loss, 7, 14, 19, 31, 37, 39
dizziness and fainting, 40

E

eating disorders, 8
extreme dieting, 37, 39

F

family therapy, 53
fat talk, 27, 36
food rituals, 39

G

genetics, 22
group therapy, 53

H

healthy eating habits, 8, 50
hospitalization, 49

I

ideal weight, 36
infertility, 15

K

kidney failure, 15, 17, 45

L

lanugo (fine hair), 14, 40

M

menstrual cycle, 14, 15, 40
muscle weakness, 40
music therapy, 50

N

National Association of Anorexia Nervosa and Associated Disorders (ANAD), 12

O

obsessive-compulsive disorder (OCD), 21
OSFED (Other Specified Feeding and Eating Disorder), 8, 12
osteoporosis, 16

P

physical exam, 48–49
prescription medicine, 49–50
psychotherapy, 50

R

recovery plan, 47–49, 53

S

self-esteem, 13, 14, 28, 29, 50
self-help, 53
self test, 44
serotonin, 21–22
skin problems, 40
social phobia, 20
social worker, 48
sports, 34, 36

T

therapist, 47, 50, 51, 53
therapy, 49, 50, 51–53
thinness and societal pressure, 24, 26
tooth decay, 40
treatment, 21, 49–51, 53
treatment plans, 49

W

weight loss/dieting, 7, 14, 19, 31, 37, 39

About the Authors

Katherine Walden is a researcher and writer who lives in the New York area. The author of several books for young children, she was interested to learn how the scientific understanding of anorexia has evolved over time.

Stephanie Watson has written or contributed to more than a dozen health and science books, including *Endometriosis, Encyclopedia of the Human Body: The Endocrine System, The Mechanisms of Genetics: An Anthology of Current Thought*, and *Science and Its Times*. Her work also has been featured in several health and wellness websites, including the National Library of Medicine's Medline Plus and the Rosen Health, Wellness, and Life Skills Database.

Photo Credits

Cover, p.3 © iStockphoto.com/realitybytes; pp. 6, 15 Barcroft Media/Getty Iamges; p. 9 AJPhoto/Science Source; p. 11 © Leila Cutler/Alamy; p. 13 Jasminko Ibrakovic/Shutterstock.com; p. 19 © Bubbles Photolibrary/Alamy; p. 20 © iStockphoto.com/Antonio Diaz; p. 23 Jupiterimages/Photolibrary/Getty Images; p. 25 Ovidiu Hrubaru/Shutterstock.com; p. 27 VGstockstudio/Shutterstock.com; p. 30 otnaydur/Shutterstock.com; pp. 32-33 Image Source/Digital Vision/Getty Images; p. 35 © iStockphoto.com/esolla; p. 38 asife/Shutterstock.com; p. 41 © AP Images; p. 42 Huy Lam/First Light/Getty Images; p. 46 © iStockphoto.com/Juanmonino; p. 51 BSIP/Universal Images Group/Getty Images; p. 52 Ron Levine/Photodisc/Getty Images

Photo Researcher: Nicole DiMella

5/23/16